This Orchard book
belongs to

_____

_____

_____

For Indie,
with love, Giles

For Imogen and
Brown Bear,
with love from Emma xx

ORCHARD BOOKS
338 Euston Road, London NW1 3BH
Orchard Books Australia
Level 17/207 Kent Street, Sydney, NSW 2000

First published in 2014 by Orchard Books
First published in paperback in 2014

ISBN 978 1 40832 750 0

Text © Giles Andreae 2014
Illustrations © Emma Dodd 2014

The rights of Giles Andreae to be identified as the author and of
Emma Dodd to be identified as the illustrator
of this work have been asserted by them in accordance with the
Copyright, Designs and Patents Act, 1988.

A CIP catalogue record for this book
is available from the British Library.

1 3 5 7 9 10 8 6 4 2

Printed in China

Orchard Books is a division
of Hachette Children's Books,
an Hachette UK Company.
www.hachette.co.uk

I love you baby

Giles Andreae & Emma Dodd

ORCHARD

Guess what I've got? Hip hip hooray!

A brand new baby to love all day!

Aren't I lucky? Yes, I know!

Why don't you come and say hello?

One fat tummy, tight like a drum.

Two little cheeks on one little bum!

Two little arms, and under the vest,

One little neck and a soft, warm chest.

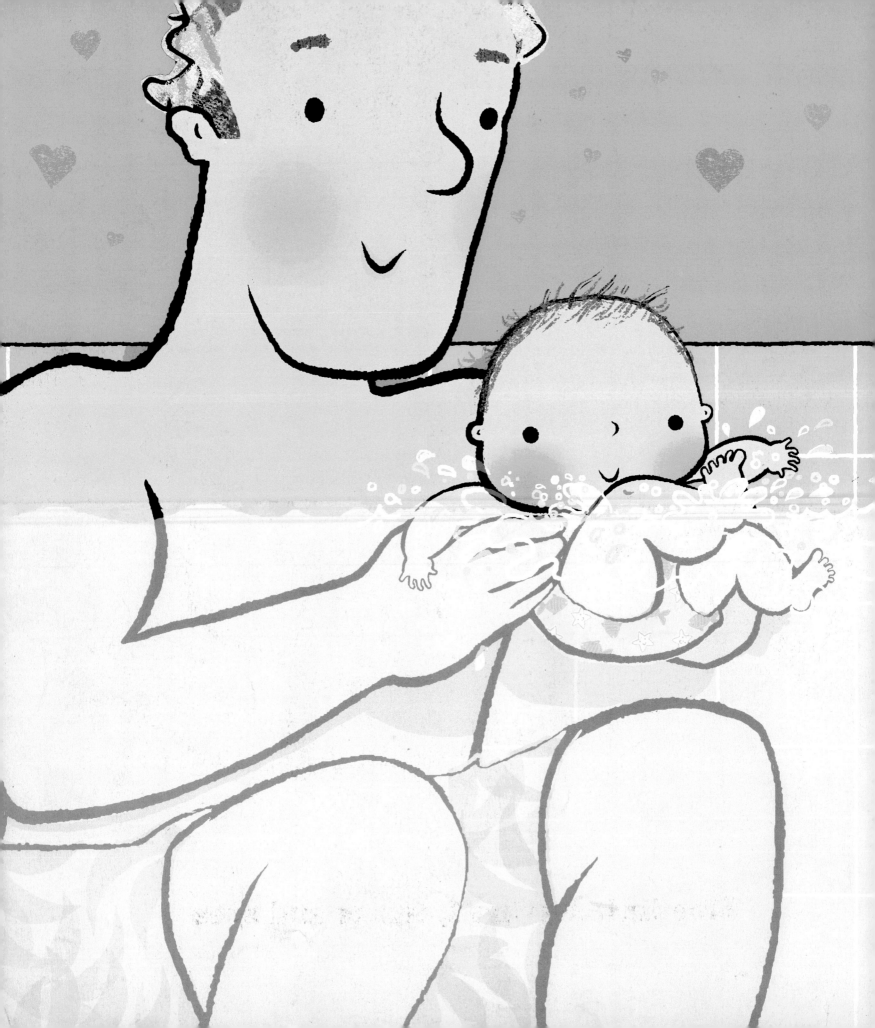

Two chubby legs and two squashy thighs.

One little forehead, two round eyes.

One funny hairstyle,
oh, what a mess!
Too many hairs for
anyone to guess.

Two tiny hands and
one small chin,

Eight squidgy knuckles

with dimples in.

Two strong shoulders,

two little wrists.

Two plump knees,

now, what have I missed?

One squishy waist and two tubby hips,

One kissy mouth with two soft lips.

Just one belly button, small and sweet,

Two pudgy ankles, two tickly feet!

Ten little fingers, ten little toes,

Two little ears and one little nose.

Two warm cheeks, all rosy and bright,

A kiss and a cuddle to say goodnight.

One sleepy face on

one sweet head,

Sleep tight, love you,
it's time for bed!